# What Mama Should Have Said

I0452177

Katrina Avant

ISBN-978-0692589830
ISBN-069258083X

**What Mama Should Have Said**
**Copyright © December 2015**
**Olivia M. Dutton**
o d u t t o n 0 1 . w i x . c o m / o l i v i a s p l a c e

**Editor**
**L.R. Clark**

**Cover Design**
**Soul Sister Ink**
K a t r i n a s w o r k s . c o m

## Taking Mama's words to heart~

**Sitting here, I can still recall many things Mama Lou said while she was teaching me and my sister through the stories of her life. It's the lessons she didn't touch on that I'm focusing on now. I know she meant well, but some things are just more important than others. But I guess with any tale there will always be some things left out—intentionally or otherwise. And it's that one particular thing she never mentioned that has landed me where I am today.**

Mama Lou is my, or should I say, was my mama. Cancer took her away from me way too soon. But before she left this world, she gave my sister and me all the wisdom she could muster about life and love. You probably think she had much to tell, but in reality, mama had limited experience when it came to life; especially when it came to relationships. The few encounters she did have, brought lessons she said needed to be taught because her mama never told her much when it came to the practicality of men. So, she collected each of those hard-won experiences and carefully placed them into a neat little box inside her soul to pass on to the next generation.

Mama Lou was a wonderful mother to me and Amber, and a good friend after we became adults. She said while children were under the age of consent, you had to treat them as such. However, that didn't stop her from getting her point across about the ways of men. She just adjusted the temperature of the talk, so to speak, with each stage in our lives. And when we turned eighteen, she turned up the heat full blast. She left nothing out; not the sex, the heartaches, nor the cheating; especially the cheating. She wanted us to fully understand what to expect when dealing with the opposite sex. She wanted us to know there were pitfalls and plenty of them.

Oh, forgive me. I'm so preoccupied with my current predicament, that I forgot to introduce myself. My name is Brianna Patrice Day, sister of Amber Nicole Day and daughter of Louise and Logan Day. Although I'm married, I refuse to take my second husband's name just as I didn't with the first one. I somehow felt I wouldn't be with him long enough to warrant such a change and I was right. I learned a great deal from Mama's tales and never fully giving into a man was at the very top of that list.

Everything Mama told us was meant for us to embrace fully and learn from, so we wouldn't repeat her mistakes. She said it was better to gain wisdom from others rather than to duplicate their sorrows. I loved that about my mama, but in my opinion, she left out some things. She never mentioned how to handle the unexpected; and better yet, how to get even when you've encountered that unexpected. So we knew the what, but not the mechanics of dealing with or preventing. She did tell us things would be complicated, whether we thought those complications were deserved or not. And after examining all the problems that have plagued me this far, I have to say I deserve them.

So, for better or worse, this is where my tale begins.

### The husband~

**Although I've only been married twice, I've had quite a few men in my life and dogged quite a few of them along the way too. But when it came to this last man, my second husband…well, you'll see.**

I believe the beginning of my woes started the day Grayson—my plaything at the time— put the car in gear and pulled away from the curb. I was so smug and satisfied with myself as I watched my husband Marc's retreating figure in the sideview mirror. He was heading back inside the house we shared together. It never ceased to amaze me how incredibly stupid the man was for someone who claimed to have had so much sense. For all of his arrogant posturing and boasting of having everything in his life in order and under control, he failed to see the one deception that was taking place right in front of his face.

Marc Hill is my second and soon-to-be former husband. And out of my two marriages, I always pegged him to be the slowest when it came to ways of true deceit. At least that's what he liked for me to believe. Even though he may not have caught on to this little charade, I discovered Marc was just as conning and conniving as the next man. And if all should be told, he just might have been better at the game than most—including me. That's saying something, considering I prided myself in knowing and breaking all the rules.

I must admit. My husband has his good traits. He's a good provider and businessman, but mostly he's what you would call a pompous ass, or what my mama called an educated fool. You know the type. Just because he had a piece of paper from some uppity university, he thought he knew everything about everything. This bigheaded attitude of his turned more people off than not. Marc was too full of himself to notice when people were shining him on. His so-called friends and business colleagues tolerated him because he was good at making them money. If it hadn't been for that, they would have soon moved on.

When Marc first started throwing around his big words and fancy sentences, I thought it was his way of impressing me or just showing off in front of his associates. But as time went on, I realized it was his arrogant way of berating me and trying to keep me in my 'place', because I didn't have a piece of paper of my own.

He started these little jabs whenever we would entertain some of his equally snooty friends. He would 'jokingly' mention my lack of a degree and call me 'the little woman' a lot, as if I didn't have a brain in my head. Somewhere in his superior little mind, he thought he was better than me. I mean he had his chest all puffed up as if some ink scratchings on a piece of parchment made it so. He would've pushed the issue further and harsher too, if I hadn't come from money. So there were times when I had to firmly remind him I was just as good as he was because of it; degree or not. That arrogance of his quickly turned me off. It was one of many reasons why I grew to despise him.

Marc's conceit was a considerable thorn in my ass, true enough. But my loving husband's eye for the ladies was the whole damn thorny rose bush. At the time I started cheating on him, his eye was on that silly personal assistant of his and had been since the day she started "working" for him. The only reasons I could see him hiring her, was for her sizable ass and generous chest, because that tramp was too lazy to talk, let alone get any real work done.

She never completed a full name. I was always Bria never Brianna. I couldn't decide if she was slow or if she was just that lazy. I would've been offended if my name had been the only one she cut off, but she did that to everyone, including Marc. Just like I was Bria, he was just plain ol' Mar. Annoying as it was, he didn't seem to mind. And that's because he was always about two drinks shy of having that big ass of hers turned up in some cheap motel room, banging her brains out. There wasn't a time when he didn't eye that cow as if she was his favorite flavored lollipop that he was dying to suck on. I long suspected he would have done her the second he hired her if everyone hadn't been privy to his fascination with her, including me. He was just that open about it. But let him tell it, his actions around her were harmless. Yeah, well…

Not only was my husband hot for her, but ol' girl was just as hot for him. Always grinning up in his face at every chance she got with him eating it up. I watched them play their little hoe-ass games when they thought I wasn't looking. The last time they thought they were being slick was at a birthday party I threw for him at his office. While everyone else was enjoying cake and champagne, those two were over in a corner with their heads together; him grinning like a satisfied cat and her kee-kee-keying like some empty-headed chicken.

Whenever anyone jokingly brought up Marc's roving eye (and many had noticed), he would wholeheartedly admit to it, but not without ceremoniously pulling me to his side; planting a kiss to a cheek; all the while claiming I was his one and only. Then the fool would raise his right hand like some over-the-hill boy scout; swearing he would never step outside our marriage. And at the time, this may have been true. But just in case it wasn't, I was already one up on his flirting ass. There was no way in hell I was going to let any man get one over on me without some counter-action. My mama may have gotten hoodwinked, but this woman right here—no, no, she ain't going. Yeah, Marc is my second husband, but given how this marriage has unraveled, he most definitely will be my last.

## Where the drama started~

**You might wonder why I have such a negative view of my husband, or men in general for that matter. Well, my view of men had been greatly shaped by my mama's woes and finished up with my own personal calamities. Before getting to my own drama, let me tell you a little bit about my mama's.**

Louise Day—aka Mama Lou—only had a total of three men in her entire lifetime and each of them did her in, one way or another. Mama Lou's first is what I consider an experiment, which I feel all women's first encounter with sex is. Some experiences are good, others not so good. Mama said her first time was so terrible that she wanted to swear off sex forever.

Now I must admit; my first encounter may have been bad, but not bad enough to just say no to a second try at it. Yeah, looking back, it could have been better; much better. I mean, the boy was so all about that thang, he didn't

bother to take his clothes off. He just unzipped; took a leg

out of my panties and shoved it in; pulled it out and it was

done. No muss no fuss. If it hadn't been for the wetness

that seeped out of me, I would have wondered if we did it

at all. Not only was he super quick, he was super small; so

small I don't think I really felt him.

But to give him a little credit; the quickness of it all

could have been due to the fact he had a steady girlfriend at

the time. While he was dry humping me in the back seat of

his car, (he considered this foreplay), he fully expected her

to show up and start breaking out windows or something.

When he was getting into his car to come pick me up, she

attempted several tries at climbing into the passenger seat,

but he managed to lock her out. The girl was so determined

to stop him, he drove off with her still clutching the door

handle. He said she held on too, until he rounded a corner

and she finally had to let go or fall face first into the street.

I guess she sensed he was about to commit treachery and tried her best to put a stop to it. Humph, and to think his sorry ass attempt at sex was my reward for all that trouble.

But getting back to Mama Lou. Her second bad occurrence was due to plain ol' ignorance and inexperience on her part. She didn't do her research to see if the man was married or not. This relationship was with some foreign guy Mama had the hots for that ended in a lukewarm uproar. I say lukewarm because the situation could have been a whole lot hotter if the guy's wife and been packing heat instead of an acid tongue; cussing mama out in some language she didn't understand.

And then there was my daddy, Logan Day. Mama claimed he was a good man, right up until he ran off with her skank-ass best friend. The skank's snatch must have been mighty good too, because he never came home again. And fortunately or unfortunately—I never decided which— this all took place before I was born. Mama found out she was pregnant with me a couple of days after Daddy left. The man never even bothered to drop in once to meet the daughter he ran out on. I guess you can say this is the real reason I have such low regards for the opposite sex. At least that's what my therapist tells me and she might be right.

So Mama's two out of three suitors were cheaters. One cheated with Mama and the other cheated on her. Cheats, cheats, cheats. As far as I'm concerned they all cheat.

But to be fair, my first husband—God rest his soul—really didn't get a chance to cheat. Sam was too busy stacking as much cash as he could. I doubt another woman was ever on his mind. That man spent the entirety of our three-year marriage chasing his real love—money. He was obsessed with it. I believe it gave him a hard-on just thinking about it. So in a way, he did have a mistress, just not the two-legged kind with a vagina.

My Sam was a hustler. Any venture he could take on to make money he would tackle it. It didn't much matter what it was. If it was legal, (although I suspected there were a few times it wasn't), and money was to be had, he was on it. That scripture about the love of money being the root of all evil should have had an amendment to it about being fatal because I truly believe it led to Sam's demise.

As a man, Sam felt he had something to prove. You see, my daddy's death, (it happened while his mistress's head was bobbing up and down between his legs), left my mama well off. And after she passed on, me and my sister inherited that wealth. So in Mr. Samuel McFarland's mind, in order to be 'the man' of the house, he had to outdo me financially, which would have taken some doing. I have to give him his props though. He worked his little heart until it literally gave out on him. Late one night, Sam had a fatal heart attack at his desk when he should have been home taking care of the real business that was between the sheets with me.

Did I cheat on Sam? Well, yeah, briefly. And I'm sure you can probably guess it was Sam's obsession with that all mighty dollar that led me to stray. I had no understanding of why a man who had a fine and sexy wife at home, willing to do most anything between the sheets, wanted to stay at the office and conduct business. Mind you, I was willing to do most, anything to keep us happy. Hell, I had needs that should have been met and Sam just wasn't cutting it. A girl has to do what a girl has to do. That affair might have been short, but it was oh, so sweet. What made it sweet? Well, that will have to be a story for another time. But I will say this; the experience will be one I will treasure for a lifetime.

Anyway, there is another reason I don't trust men to do the right thing. Remember me telling you about being in the car with Grayson? Well, he's just one more reason I don't trust the male species. I might have been cheating on my husband with him, but he knew up front I was married and was willing to take me on anyway. Just goes to show; none of them can be trusted.

#

Grayson was so bold to pick me up in front of my house while my husband was home. But don't let this sway you, because it wasn't as it appeared; not quite. And to prove my point, when I looked over at him that day, I burst into complete hysteria. The sight of him brought about laughter so strong, it brought tears to my eyes. Grayson didn't have to ask what was so funny. He just looked at me and grinned that sexy, sly grin of his.

Humph. All I can do is shake my head at Grayson's antics. The things that man was willing to do, just to be with me, still takes my breath away.

You see, Grayson, my lover, was dressed in a woman's blouse and a long blond wig; complete with full make-up, all courtesy of his sister Marlene. And the biggest kicker? Grayson and Marlene are my husband's first cousins, and at the time, neither one of them could stand him. For that matter, Marc had gotten on my nerves too; hence me sneaking out of the house for a booty call with cousin Grayson.

You might ask why I bothered to get married in the first place since I didn't seem to take matrimony seriously. Well, I guess somewhere in the back of my mind, I still longed for a man who was honest and true; but at the same time, I felt it wasn't possible to find such a man. I was doing what Mama called wishing and betting. Wishing I could find a good solid man, but betting I wouldn't. I think my sister and I had the same philosophy about relationships. That was just how we rolled. And if you think I was bad…oohwee! Well, I'll just let Amber tell her own story if she chooses to do so.

Any who, a girl gets lonely even if she does know the game. After all, why should I punish myself by not having a steady and proper bed partner just because men cheat? Anyway, that was how I used to feel. Now, I'm not so sure about anything I've done up to this point.

## A little more background~

**Now, Mama Lou had her points when it came to dealing with men. I will give her that. But under the circumstances, what she should have said was, get them before they get you. And like it or not, this is the viewpoint I lived by, which is where Grayson fits into all this.**

Grayson Hill and I met shortly after Marc and I celebrated our first wedding anniversary and we had been seeing each other on a regular basis until recently. By the time we met, I had just about had enough of my husband's shenanigans and Grayson fit the bill perfectly. I often wondered if I'd met Grayson first, would there have been a need for cheating—at least that's how I saw it back then. Grayson was something special; different than most of the guys I'd been with.

My husband's cousin was every woman's dream; smart, handsome, and rich in his own right. Where he and Marc may have shared these similar characteristics, as well as a last name, that's where the comparison stopped. Where Marc was stuffy and uptight, Grayson was carefree and fun-loving. He loved living on the edge; walking that sharp razor line between what's right and what's wrong. We did things together that Marc found to be a waste of time, like having sex in risqué places. We could do it anywhere anytime, it didn't matter. The more erotic and daring the better.

Marc's idea of fun was planning out every move before he made one step. Grayson flew by the seat of his pants and always landed on his feet, no matter what. Spontaneity was his middle name. When I was with him, I never knew what I was in for. No matter the adventure, there was always a satisfying ride that ended in mind-blowing climaxes. Who could ever think spontaneity as a waste of time? Don't get me wrong, my husband had his moments, but they were so few and far between, I almost forgot those moments ever existed.

When Marc was fun, we did a lot of things together. At the start of fall, we would take my baby girl Sasha—my daughter from my first marriage—and drive along the countryside in search of a good spot for picnics. The fall season was both of our favorites. We would hike through the beautifully colored trees and just enjoy the clear open outdoors. On those occasions when Sasha wasn't with us, we would make love on a bed of those colorful autumn leaves. For me, the clean, crisp air outside of the city was a natural aphrodisiac that always put me in the mood, and Marc was always in the right frame of mind to satisfy. In those days, he and I used to take long weekend getaways together just to enjoy each other's company.

But at some point, Marc had come to believe having wealth meant not having any real fun, at least not with me.

After a while, just like Sam, wealth became more and more his focus. Having Sam die on me taught me a lesson. Any man that came after him had to have money too. I didn't need another husband dropping dead on me, chasing after that green mistress. I thought marrying a man already established financially would end that need for more. I was wrong. I never thought trading in for dollars would exclude everything else. Marc may have been home a lot physically, but at times, his mind was on other things. And at the time, I thought that meant business, but somewhere among our many dinner parties social gatherings, and even lovemaking, Marc had become boring and controlling.

## Tit for Tat~

**I told you how my husband could turn people off with his arrogance. Well, Marc mistakenly thought his degrees gave him a license to control every part of our lives.**

I may have overseen the household, but Marc took it upon himself to oversee me. He liked to keep himself "abreast", (his word, not mine), of every detail of what was going on with me; from household chores to clocking my spare time. This peculiarity was one of the things that made him an obnoxious butt-hole who everyone eventually despised. But at the same time, this was one of the reasons I married him. I mistook this take-control trait as him being strong. I was wrong again. Being head of the household was one thing, taking it over the top was another.

Marc started with our food. I often planned meals we were used to and enjoyed eating. After a while, those weren't good enough. He wanted fancier dinners with place settings in the formal dining room every evening, instead of our usual cozy setup in the family nook in the kitchen. And since I couldn't prepare the foods he chose, he enrolled me in a gourmet cooking and etiquette class, as if I was some uncouth ghetto hood rat or something. This was another jab at me for not having gone to college.

Well, me being me, punched right back and hired a gourmet chef who provided him with the niceties he said we were lacking. And for that etiquette class, I told him he could stick it where the sun don't shine; humph, the nerve. And I'm pretty sure you can guess this didn't go over too well with my dear 'edjumicated' husband, but he got over it.

Since he didn't win that fight, he picked another one. Next came the issue of how I dressed and how I dressed Sasha. Marc wanted us to dress like royalty instead of like the everyday people we were. He bought us these fancy dresses and things, trying to transform us into something we were not. I shove every one of those pretentious frocks in a storage closet. My daughter, on the other hand, thought it was fun until some of her friends started calling her uppity, so that put an end to that. Not one to favor peer pressure, this time I applauded it. I didn't have to open my mouth one time to make my point. Sasha's friends did it for me. She may have valued Marc's advice, but she valued the sting of her friends' ridicule more.

I did not want my child going to school every day looking like she was going to meet the queen, and I sure as hell was not going to go along with his nonsense just to please him. He might have liked donning three grand suits every day and shoes that cost enough to feed a small country, but that was not how I wanted to raise my daughter and it certainly wasn't what I wanted for myself. Mama Lou had a saying for what Marc was doing. She called it 'putting on airs'. He was acting like he was something out of the ordinary; like his shit didn't stink. He got to the point where nothing was ever good enough, no matter what direction I took. If King Marc didn't sanction it, it wasn't good enough for the kingdom.

You would think he would have given up after the defeat over the clothes; but nah, not His Majesty. This is when he leveled up and started clocking my time. All of a sudden he needed to know where I was when I wasn't in his presence. Since I refused to work (and why should I?), he wanted to know what I was doing with my leisure time. I didn't have a job and Sasha was in school, so this was a problem for him. It was one thing when I did the cooking and the cleaning, but after I hired people to do those things, I had lots of free time. So much free time, he started calling me all throughout the day, just to say 'hi'. So he said. But I knew better. I think he thought I was up to no good. At this point, I wasn't, but was well on my way to getting there with a big shove from him, because of his erratic ass behavior.

This invisible leash Marc had me on lasted about a month, before I slowed his roll on that issue too. I got tired of him calling me so I made it easy for him. He wanted to know where I was, so be it. I randomly showed up at his office; strolling through that place like I owned it. At first, he thought my impromptu visits were cute, and most of Marc's employees thought so too. And as for his slow-ass assistant, not so much. My unannounced visits slowed her roll on throwing the coochie at my husband. She had to be pushing it all up in his face the way she was dressed. That tramp's clothes were so tight, that I often wondered if she could breathe.

When I high-stepped it through the office, she would put on that fake-ass smile of hers and mangle my name even more. I made it a point to make sure she was on guard duty, so I could push past her and burst up into his office. A few times I did this, Marc was in meetings with some top clients. Needless to say, my visits to the office weren't so cute anymore. Interrupting him at work, and in front of his colleagues, soon put a stop to the visits and the check-up calls home. He finally realized he wasn't dealing with an amateur. When he served me tit, I sure as hell volleyed back with a tat. Problem solved!

## Enter the sideman~

**It was shortly after slam dunking Marc's choke hold on me that I took up with Grayson, wig, and all.**

Mama Lou had it right when she said to make sure we weren't done in by a man. Well, those may not have been her exact words, but that's what I got out of her many speeches. I know she meant for me to be vigilant at all times; to catch the signs they gave when things weren't quite right. And I know she probably would have viewed my treatment of Marc as harsh, and she would have been right. But the way I saw it, I had no other choice, considering how Daddy did her in the end. I did not want that to be me.

I loved my mama when she was still with us, and I still do. But there should have been more fire to the way she handled Daddy and herself. When he ran off with that woman, she should have found him and beat his cheating ass and then found herself a replacement the moment she finished. I think she let Daddy slide away a little too easily with that skank Evil. That's the nickname Mama gave her so-called best friend Eva after she took my daddy away from us.

I was there that night when Mama finally kicked her betraying ass. Daddy had just died and ol' Evil had shown up at our door for some sympathy and a handout. My mama gave her a hand alright, and it wasn't what she was looking for either. Because we were young, my sister and I may not have understood exactly what happened between the two of them, but we knew it had to be monumental for our sweet, passive mother to wail on Evil's ass. That was the first and last time I ever saw Mama Lou act out. And looking back, it had been well overdue.

But getting back to why Grayson was dressed like a woman. Marc and this is according to his sad, sorry ass, has only one flaw—his weak eye-sight. His eyes were too weak for contact lenses so that meant he needed glasses. And being the vain man that he is, he refused to wear them unless he was reading over some contract. Couldn't have him squinting over legal documents, no sir. He might miss a dollar or two if he did that. And there was one more occasion when he wore them. He always made sure they were perched on the end of his nose when he wanted to let his eyes crawl all over that slow cow's backside.

Anyhow, when Grayson and I first started fooling around, we used his sister Marlene as our go-between. We had to. Marc may have stopped my office visits and his frequent checkup calls, but he was still trying to clock my every movement. Cousin Marlene changed all that.

Marlene would come to dinner every other night; just enough to get Marc used to having her around. He didn't mind. In fact, he encouraged her visits. He was too tickled that I was getting along with his family to pay much attention to anything else that might have been going on.

Marc saw my friendship with Marlene, as a way to rebuild that bridge he'd burned down between them. He may not have admitted it, but he missed those family ties; and having Marlene around proved—in his mind—that his cousins had forgiven him. He had messed things up with them years ago. And the plus for me was his letting go of the reins he tried wrapping around my neck.

Since Marlene was my link to her brother, it may look like I was just using her, but it wasn't that way at all. She and I were friends then, and better friends now. I like Marlene. She's been the type of friend all women should have during times of crisis. Back then, she got something out of our association too. And what did she get out of this sordid pact? The satisfaction of knowing someone was knocking her smart-ass cousin down a peg or two, whether he was aware of it or not.

After our dinners became successful, Marlene started coming around to get me for 'girls' night out'; or if we were really bold, girls' weekend away. We would make sure to plan our retreats at the dinner table, with Marc grinning like a fool in agreement. The trips were always to Marlene's spa in Virginia. Visiting one of her spas was how we met in the first place. Marc had sent me there for a complete beauty makeover for our wedding. Looking back on that, I wonder if he thought I was 'lacking' in that area too. This would have been absurd, considering my mama and daddy—without a doubt—made a beauty when they made me.

Well anyway, after Marlene discovered who I was marrying, she thought I would need a friend sooner or later and kept in touch. And boy was she right. After Marc started acting a fool, I started making regular visits to the spa in town, just to catch a breather from his annoying ass. It was on one of my visits when she introduced me to her brother, and we hit it off immediately— with Marlene's approval of course.

On the days Marlene and I had our 'outings', with her insisting on driving, she would pull up to the front of the house and text me when she was outside. I would sweetly kiss my husband goodbye and drive off with his blessing. But In reality, Marlene would take me to meet up with Grayson and go on her merry way. But after a while, this wasn't good enough for Grayson. He wanted to push things to the edge, as only he could do. Like I said before, he's a risk-taker. He decided he wanted to pick me up himself and this is where Marlene's help came in handy again.

Because Marc's eyesight was so bad, she was the one who suggested the disguise. She started by putting one of her wigs on Grayson and adding a little lipstick, just in case Marc was within squinting distance when Grayson pulled up to the house in her car. I must say. I was floored the first time he showed up in that getup. And what made it more edgy, Marc just happened to be in the yard that evening; absently giving 'Marlene' an approving wave before heading back inside the house. Grayson's crazy ass boldly waved right back. All Marc saw was the blur of Marlene's bleached blond wig and fire engine red lipstick; never once guessing it was actually a man behind the wheel. And certainly never guessing it was Grayson.

I held my breath that day; praying Marc wouldn't walk me to the car to say hello or we were busted. And I didn't release that breath until we were nearly three blocks away and out of Marc's flawed sight. I remember Grayson chasing the tension away, by sliding his capable hand under my skirt to my sweet spot. Soon that man had me moaning and grinding without another thought of blind Marc. As Grayson brought me to climax, he just grinned. He too was loving the fact he was 'sticking it' to his cousin, literally and figuratively.

## The ties that bind~

**I know you're wondering why Grayson and Marlene hate my husband so. Well, let me give you a little history on the Hill family ties, or in this case broken bonds.**

Marc, Grayson, and Marlene all grew up together. The cousins are a product of two brothers who competed in everything they did; somewhat passing this ugliness down to their offspring. And I say somewhat because, over the years, Marc would be the only one who would keep that foolishness going.

Like with my first husband, the senior Hills worked hard at outdoing each other in every part of their lives. Competing until their very last breaths. They both died in a horrific crash onboard their private jet. From what I've been told by Marlene, the two were bickering over who should have been flying the damn plane, and not paying attention to the mountain that was rushing towards them.

Well, after that calamity, Marlene and Grayson saw the handwriting on the wall and promptly bowed out of the family rivalry, leaving the unpopular familial practice to Marc. Where he thrived on this dissension, Grayson and Marlene found the competition with their cousin foolishness for all involved. It was just too exhausting and too demeaning for the siblings to compete with a know-it-all butt-hole, so they just stopped. And like any self-absorbed idiot, Marc took this as a sign of weakness and doubled down on rubbing their noses in whatever venture he was making a killing. The fool didn't have sense enough to realize the cousins were making pretty good themselves. They just chose not to crow about it.

Marlene owns a chain of full-service beauty spas, all up and down the eastern seaboard, from New York City down through the Carolinas, with future plans of opening in

Miami. You can choose to pamper yourself for a day pass or spend a weekend getting every part of your body whipped and fluffed into shape. Marlene's love for the industry grew from an early age. Her mama started taking her to spas as soon as she was old enough to walk. Mama Hill thought it was important for a lady to be properly groomed at all times. So when Marlene was old enough to earn her own money, she invested in her first salon; hiring the best people for the services they provided. From there she started growing an empire.

But unbeknownst to most people, (including my husband), Marlene later added a more intimate service that profited her more money in a week than her other services netted in a month. Marlene Hill ran an upscale escort service, secretly headquartered in her number one day spa here in New York City. When I say upscale I do mean upscale.

The escorts she employs are the crème de la crème of beautiful people; all treated and serviced by the spa, as part of their employment package. And since her clientele is the top shelf of society, their mutual association cushions her from any blows that might have been hurled her way by any branch of the legal system.

Her employees aren't just women either. Most think of men patronizing these particular services, but she has her fair share of female clients too. Her customers include governors, senators, foreign dignitaries, and the police commissioner. And whether it's known by them or not, some of the wives of these men are playing in this particular playground also. These people, who are all dignified and upright in public, are partakers of fleshly delights behind closed doors. So it was in Marlene's best interest to discontinue her participation in Marc's sadistic little game. This particular branch of her business could never be known publicly. And knowing Marc, if for a

second he thought Marlene was outdoing him, he would
have found a way to out her just for the sadistic hell of it.

While Marlene held the golden key to the kingdom
of flesh, her brother took a totally different route. After
college, Grayson followed his sister's hunger for
entrepreneurship and started his own construction firm that
has its headquarters here in the city also, with satellite
offices around the world. It seems he has a knack for
building beautiful structures that people pay good money
for. And with him raking in all that cash, it affords him
anything he wants, but you wouldn't know it by the way he
acts and dresses. Where Marc likes to spend mega bucks on
clothes and cars and such, Grayson prefers his jeans and a
simple Mercedes, without all the bells and whistles. He said
those material things just never appealed to him.

Grayson loves his life and what he does for a living.
They both do. But my husband would never acknowledge
either of their successes; not to their faces anyway.

According to him, they could have done better than beauty shops and construction sites. It's just like the butt-hole; never giving credit where credit is due. He'd rather keep up the competition where only he is competing.

It was Marc's nasty competitive behavior that eventually created the rift between Grayson and Marlene. Because of this, the siblings won't have anything to do with that side of their family. They didn't even attend our wedding because of Marc's asinine ways. They knew he would find a way to rub their noses in that too, considering neither of them had a spouse of their own. Marc prided himself on being the first in everything. So his marriage to me was just one more thing he could add to his ever-growing list of 'I'm better than you' deeds.

But Marc's put-downs didn't bring as much joy as he thought it would. Before I came along, the cousins weren't even speaking to each other, let alone socializing together. Grayson still won't have much to do with him. So when Marlene started showing up at the house, he was actually relieved, whether he would admit to that fact or not. I felt it was good for Marc to have some contact with his relatives, even if it was under false pretenses. At any rate, Marlene's presence kept him off my back. The way I saw it, it was a big win for everybody.

### How It All Began~

**Things weren't always bad between me and my husband. In fact, things were quite good between us in the beginning.**

I met Marc shortly after my mama passed away, and it had been a few years since I'd buried my first husband. Although there had been some men friends in between, they were just a few insignificant encounters nothing serious. I hope I don't sound like some cat in heat; on the prowl after Sam died, because it wasn't like that at all. I just happened to be up for a little male company every now and then. Anyway, by the time I met Marc, I was in between company keepers.

Marc was in real estate like my daddy, owning several businesses and brownstones around Strivers Row where we lived. I'd heard his name around the way but never met the man. I never had a reason to. But when

Amber and I decided to sell both Mama's and our Aunt Johnnie Mae's brownstones, Marc was recommended as the person to go to. His collection of brownstones was his pride and joy. He would buy up blocks of them and turn them into beautiful showplaces and sell them for huge profits. And depending on the agreement with the seller, and if the property was well kept beforehand, the seller got a piece of the turnaround, making it a win for everyone involved.

Well, Amber couldn't meet with him that day so we agreed I would make the initial contact alone. When I met him, there was no love or lust at first sight. My second husband didn't just jump off the page, so to speak, in the attracting department. I wasn't looking for that anyway. I'd just lost Mama Lou and wasn't in the right frame of mind for receiving company, as she used to say.

Marc was nice enough. We talked about how to proceed in selling the two places; all the while I could tell he was interested in more than my brownstones. He smiled a lot with good teeth. Something I always look for in a man. There is nothing worse than having a man open his mouth and some of his teeth were crooked, buttered, or just plain gone. That was a deal breaker.

After we discussed money and a possible deal—Amber had to put her stamp of approval on it first—he asked if he could see me some time. I didn't give him a direct answer then, because like I said, I was still grieving and was trying to slow my roll on my company keeping. Plus, I had my young daughter to think of.

Sasha was coming to that age where she was beginning to figure things out about my company, and I couldn't have that. That was why I put the brakes on the men I entertained in the first place. That story Mama Lou told us about her spying on her neighbors growing up, had me spooked a bit where my own daughter was concerned. I didn't need my Sasha peeping in on me through keyholes or stuff like that. Some things children need not learn at an early stage in life. Unlike Mama, I didn't want my daughter to know too much too soon. Sometimes I think Mama Lou told me and Amber a little too much. Needless to say, it took him several weeks of trying, before I accepted his invitation to dinner.

I'll never forget our first date. That man was dressed to the nines and was as fancy as you please with his flowers, chocolates, and a case of expensive wine. He even brought a gift for my child. Now, I wasn't no slouch in receiving company. Mama Lou made sure of that. She told me and Amber that no man should come for a visit with empty hands. And if one did, send him packing, because he had nothing to offer but a wet ass. The word ass is my touch. Mama Lou was more ladylike in her description.

But getting back to Mark. Not only was his hands not empty, but this man had gone out of his way to impress me. My usual company would only bring a bottle of something—usually brown liquor, which by the way I don't drink—and a pat on the head for my daughter, if she happened to be up. I didn't mind. Those jokers weren't there for keeps; just long enough to get my rocks off, if you know what I mean.

If I thought Marc's initial gesture was impressive, I was in for a shocker. He didn't stop at the first date gifts, no ma'am. He made a bigger display, by taking me to one of the most eloquent and expensive restaurants in Manhattan; complete with seven-course meals and fine champagne. And after dinner, he took me on a carriage ride around Central Park. I must admit I was more than impressed. I felt special and valued. Something I hadn't felt in a long time.

I have to admit; that not feeling valued part in my other 'relationships', was my fault. There is something to be said about a woman having her own money. Sometimes it tends to lower your standards and expectations. Because I had my own moola, I never required much from the men I fooled around with. What they couldn't or wouldn't provide, I could get for myself. It also was a way for me to stay in control. If I didn't need anything from them, I could use them and get rid of them fast and easy. So it was a delight that Marc took time to impress me; something I didn't even know I needed. And I guess that's why I fell into bed with him the moment he saw me home after our date. I'd forgotten all about limiting my company keeping. But believe me; the man was well worth the compromise.

Still not ready for anything exclusive, we dated some and got to know each other more. Marc had his good qualities—sex being a good portion of them—and bad like most folks. Apart from the sex, one of the more interesting draws for me was his business sense. That man could take a dollar and turn it into a pile before you knew it. I even gave him a few of my own dollars which he multiplied in no time. The man was a money-making machine and he knew it. Most of his confidence was tied to his head for business, which led to greater confidence in using his other head in the bedroom. Yes, yes, I know. I tend to circle back to that. But if you had experienced what I had, you would focus on that too.

Marc was extra special in the bedroom. That man had a way with his penis that made you forget about everything else. By all standards, you wouldn't think so, with his all work and no play façade; a very deceiving façade, because the man could lay down some lovin'.

Please don't get me wrong. It's not that he wasn't attractive, because he was. It was just that he was a bit of a tight ass too. Sometimes he would take things way too seriously. In my opinion, he needed to learn the art of sarcasm and lightheartedness, to get along better with people. It had been my experience, that men who were that uptight weren't much good in the sex department, but Marc proved that theory wrong; which at times, made him well worth the trouble.

But the thing that sealed the deal for me, as far as making him a keeper, was his way with my baby girl. You would have thought he was the child's father the way he carried on. Marc was patient and kind with her. It was these times when that uptight veneer of his would drop from his character. It was like he completely understood her young mind and could work on her level. He would even take time to help her with school projects and answer any questions she had. No one had ever done that before. Like I said, my other male friends never had more than a pat on the head for my daughter. And that was because they were too preoccupied with thoughts of laying me between the sheets to even consider interacting with her.

And my girl's interaction with Marc was just as grand. The way Sasha reacted to him you would have thought the man hung the moon. I didn't exist when he was around. Sasha was fascinated by Marc's knowledge and all the attention he gave her. You have to remember, her daddy died when she was little, so she never had that caring daddy part in her life. And since Marc didn't have any children of his own, they took to each other like ducks to water. I could see where he would be a good father, as well as a suitable mate. So while Marc was planning his next business move, I was plotting on how to hook him as my next husband.

We got married on a Sunday with my sister Amber standing up for me, and my baby girl grinning proudly as our flower girl. Marc had one of his business associates to stand up for him. I realized later that his personality didn't attract too many people to consider him a friend. It was a beautiful day and we made the most of it. Marc arranged for the wedding reception to be an elegant outdoor event at the restaurant from our first date. There were violinists, special chefs, and waiters to attend to our guests' every need; and the food? My Lord, it was beyond delicious. Marc spared no expense for our special day.

I was happy; making my rounds; laughing and greeting guests. I was happy until I spotted my new husband grinning at the hostess. That might not have been a problem if I hadn't also spotted him squeezing her generous behind when he thought no one was looking. With folded arms, I waited for the heffa to slap him for being fresh. But she grinned like she was used to that sort of behavior from him. She even winked at him before leaving to continue her hostess duties. Needless to say, my happy, joyous demeanor had turned to sour mash.

Now don't get me wrong. Just because I was married didn't mean I had let my guard down when it came to my new husband. I just thought we would've made it past the wedding day before he started his shenanigans. I just shook my head. I didn't let it get to me though. I just sighed and continued to play the happy bride. It didn't make sense to act a fool then and mess up everyone's happy time. So I made up my mind to deal with Marc's treachery later.

And later I did. We were in the bridal suite, at some fancy hotel he had chosen for us when I let him have it. From his reaction, you would've thought I'd slapped him across the face when I brought up his ass-squeezing session with that hostess. That man sputtered and stuttered until he couldn't come up with a reasonable lie to wiggle out of it. Surrendering, he claimed no contest against the charge and begged for my forgiveness. I forgave him; right before proclaiming there would be no pussy, as a just punishment for his misdeeds. Needless to say, there was no consummation of the marriage that night.

## In a good place ~

**After that foolishness at the wedding reception and the confrontation on our wedding night, things moved along.**

It took me two weeks before I would allow my new husband to touch me. This was just as hard on me as it was on him. Sleeping in the same bed every night next to a man you know can lay it down right is torture. But I had to make my point up front, so he'd know not to play with me in the future. I had to let him know there would be consequences if he ever disrespected me like that again. Even though I'd forgiven him, I'd made up in my mind that he wasn't to be trusted from that point on.

After we finally got the lovin' on, we set ourselves into a smooth and easy routine. Marc would go off to the office to make a living for us, and I played Lady of the Manor. And when I say manor, I do mean manor. Marc moved us into one of the oldest and wealthiest neighborhoods in the area. Our home was grand, to say the least, with its winding staircase and intricately decorated rooms. Personally, I would have been just fine in one of the townhouses in Harlem, but he said he'd always wanted a home with a manicured lawn and circular drive. He said it was important that 'our' baby girl had a proper place to entertain when she invited her friends over. Not to mention the grand parties he was planning on giving.

Businesswise, Marc had moved up in the ranks and had become a mover and a shaker in his circle of entrepreneurs. So for him, appearances were important in displaying the right financial background. For himself, he chose the finest of tailored suits and bought us showy, expensive cars, to prove our worthiness in that particular circle. I was used to nice things, but the kind of money he spent just wasn't my cup of tea. He even hired a tutor and a nanny for my baby girl, because the others in the circle had them for their children.

Don't get me wrong, we could afford all of these amenities, I just didn't see the point of it all. Mama Lou always said, sometimes you needed just a little to get by. I might not have agreed with his need for performing as grand master of the estate, or for me playing the lady of the manor for that matter, but it was his money he was spending. Before we got married, we drew up an agreement saying his money was his and mine was mine. That was just fine with me. I didn't need his money. Remember, I was rich in my own rite.

The one financial concern we did share was that of Sasha's schooling, which was a high-dollar private one. Amber and I went to public school and we turned out just fine. But because we grew up, according to Mama Lou, 'well off', I didn't see the need to invest time in higher learning to get anywhere else in life, even though my mama held a degree herself. On the other hand, my sister took to higher education like our mama did, and gained herself a Master's degree in this, that, and the other. That was fine for her; it just wasn't for me. Mama never pushed, but left the door open if I wanted to go to college.

After watching Amber rise in the ranks in her own field, with her girl wanting to follow in her footsteps, I wanted Sasha to have a college education too. So Marc and I figured, if we surrounded her with other children with that goal, she would be more apt to go herself. Marc had a couple of college degrees and made good use of them. He even suggested that I go back to school to get one of my own. But the thing was, I had no interest in doing anything. At this revelation is when he started the whole looking down his nose at me thing until I put him in his place. That was something Sam never did to me, even though he too went to college.

There was another difference between Marc and my first husband. Marc knew when to quit working at the end of the day. He was usually home every evening by six come what may. He said what couldn't be done between the hours of eight to five could wait another day. He wanted to spend time with his family and spend time growing his family. As I mentioned, he took to Sasha like she was his own, but he longed to have a son to carry on his name. And believe me, that man spent just about every waking moment we had together, trying to make one. But I failed to tell him I was on the pill and had no plans to stop taking them.

There were two reasons why I held on to my birth control with a death grip. The first reason involved Marc himself. I didn't want any ties to him when it came time to part ways. I may have been foolish enough to have a child with my first husband, but he had the good sense to die before it became an issue.

The other reason came when I started fooling around with Grayson. We were always doubled up—me with my pills and him with the condoms. I wasn't taking any chances. I refused to be one of those women you saw on those talk shows, who had gotten herself pregnant and didn't know who the father was. Can you see me with child and wondering if it was my husband's or my lover's? No ma'am and no sir, that was not going to happen to me.

Poor Marc, he tried his best to sex up on a baby. We could be having a dinner party with guests wandering all over the place, and he would have me in one of the many powder rooms going at it. That was one of the things I liked about him. He wasn't shy about what he wanted or when he wanted it. That man has had me all over our house; in every nook and every cranny; and in every conceivable position. So you see, me cheating on him had nothing to do with him not giving me any attention, it was all about me not trusting him from our wedding day and his asinine behavior. Some have said that he wasn't inclined to cheat, because he was sexing me so much and so good that I could've just overlooked his funky attitude. Well, that was their opinion. But I didn't care to consider it back then and I certainly don't agree with it now; and with good reason. I will tell you more about that later.

'We' tried making us a son for nearly two years without success. You would have thought this would have upset Marc, especially since it was his mission to make this happen. But he seemed to be fine with the raunchy acts without the results. But by this time, he had some new business ventures on his plate that were taking his company to the next level, and out of town a few days out of the month. He was looking to expand into more cities with his real-estate projects; and in order to do this, he hired more office staff to get the job done.

One of the new hires was his newest right-hand man, or should I say woman; a bow-hipped, high-yellow girl who looked like she just came out of middle school instead of grad school. His other girl was still in play, but this girl here had special duties, which required her to be at his side more than that lazy ass administrative assistant of his. He might have bumped ol' girl up to the next level if he hadn't finally realized she really was slow. He could have easily replaced her with someone more competent. But because she had been with him for so long, he didn't have the heart to fire her. He had a point. Who else would've taken her?

Kelly wasn't a problem at first. That was the new girl's name. After Marc introduced us, I didn't even give her a second thought. I saw her as no threat because I knew my husband. Miss Kelly Clay was much too young for the likes of Marc Hill. Marc, with his roving eye, was into women; those females who were old enough to have had some experience about life. Kelly had none.

As I mentioned before, Marc had an eye for the ladies; but they were always, always in our age group. And it wasn't like we were middle-aged or nothing; we were mid thirtyish and this child was early babyish. So I paid her no mind. She was safe from my husband. Besides, as far as I could see, Marc had stuck to our marriage vows and kept it in his pants. But I discovered it wasn't him I had to worry about. The problem came when baby girl started coming on to him.

Marc came home one evening all flustered and out of sorts. He was so agitated that I canceled my outing with Grayson. I'd never seen him like that before. When he finally told me what the problem was, I was floored. That Kelly Clay turned out to be a low-ball hoefessional in disguise. She was all 'professional' and strictly business during working hours. But Lord, let that sun drop below the horizon and she turned into something totally different. She roamed the halls of Hill's Realty looking for anything in pants she could spread her legs for, and that didn't exclude the cleaning staff. Miss Kelly's panties had burned clean off that snatch of hers. This showed to prove why a degree didn't make anyone better than me. In Kelly's case, it surely didn't guarantee any class or banish any whorish tendencies.

Marc said he'd heard the rumors circulating the office, and thought the men were just putting on, because a sweet young thang may have looked in their direction a time or two. You know how men can lie. But he was thrown for a loop when she finally circled her way around to offering him his turn. I guess she saved the boss for last.

They were wrapping up the last of some paperwork for the day when he excused himself and stepped into his private washroom. He said when he returned, Miss Thang was spread over his desk wearing nothing but an ass-inviting smile. Miss Kelly had dropped those drawers just that quick. And according to Marc, he picked up each and every piece of clothing, handed them to her then grabbed his things and left. He was too stunned to utter a word.

My husband said the girl was a little flirty, but he just took it as harmless young girl stuff. That was until he found her bent over his desk, butt-ass naked, and fully expecting him to take her as the other men had. But instead of taking the nympho-skank up on her offer, he grabbed his coat and ran for home.

Now, I looked at this situation two ways. First, this heffa needed her ass beat; and second, I was wrong about my husband. He didn't give in to this blatant display of temptation and I felt bad. I felt bad because I was cheating on him over an offense that I thought he might commit. We had been married approximately two and a half years and not one time had he stepped out of bounds. He hadn't even touched ol' Slow-Moe, (the name I finally gave his assistant), who I fully expected him to screw from the day I caught them with their heads together.

I almost wished he had nailed the skank. It would have made me feel better about what I was doing with his cousin. After I knuckled down my guilt, I still wanted to give that girl a much needed ass-whooping. I would settle my conflict over my own treachery later.

The next day I accompanied Marc to work and marched right into the girl's office, fully ready to whoop some ass, but I didn't get the chance. I searched all over the building for her, before being told by HR she had faxed in her immediate resignation; claiming the job was more than she could handle. Nah, what she couldn't handle was me beating her down if I had gotten a hold of her hot ass. You may wonder why I bothered since I was the one stepping out. Well, if I hadn't acted all indignant, my husband would have been looking at me sideways and I couldn't have that. At some point, I knew I would have to settle my debts in that department.

Anyway, after talking to Lucy in HR is when I discovered the girl had screwed every man in the building, but my husband. This made me feel even more guilt-ridden. At that point, I wanted to stop seeing Grayson. I had been completely wrong about my husband all along. I wouldn't have ever believed it, but there was a man out there who could just say no.

That day I took assessment of my life and the situation I had created for myself. Nothing about my hand in our marriage was fair; not to Marc and not to my daughter. Although Sasha never saw the devious side of me, I began to feel bad on her account too. Was this how I wanted my daughter to see relationships? Did I really want her to turn into a replica of me? The more I questioned myself on Sasha's behave, the more I felt like scum. I was wrong and there was no way I could justify my actions.

Even though Marc and I never fought or raised our voices toward one another, she had to feel the disconnected sham that was masquerading as our marriage. Sure we still made love and were cordial towards one another, but it could have been so much more if I had just given it a decent chance, and not branded him a liar and a cheat from the get-go. No one was perfect. Lord knows I wasn't. So why did I expect him to be?

## A change gonna come~

**After Kelly "Set My Cat on Fire" Clay left, things fell back into an easy grove and moved right along. This made it difficult to see the subtle changes that came along. The changes were so subtle, I think I missed them.**

Marc still needed a right hand, but this time he hired a man. We both breathed a little easier after Renaldo came on board. Even Slow-Moe was a bit more chipper. I discovered she didn't like Kelly's ass either. I guess you say I could call the girl by her name, but I didn't see the importance of doing that, since she didn't see the need in pronouncing mine correctly. Besides, after my husband displayed his gallant act of restraint, by not screwing Kelly, I further pushed that lazy cow to the back of my reality.

Although Marc was still expanding his territory, he still found his way home by six when he was in town. His business trips had increased, but not so much that either of us complained. He still valued our family time. When I wasn't sneaking out to play with Grayson, we had family outings just like we used to. Marc and Sasha just ate it up. I tried, but I just wasn't feeling it. Everything felt so false to me. I don't know if it was the consciousness of my behavior, or if Kelly had left something behind that I should have recognized. Something was off-center, but I just didn't know what it was.

By this time, I'd cut back on my trips with 'Marlene' and only saw Grayson two to three times a month. When we did get together, it was during the times Marc was out of town. I would make sure to arrange for Sasha to spend time with Amber and her daughter, so I could be free to partake of Grayson for as long and as much as I liked. As I said before, I was feeling guilty for my outrageous behavior, but not enough to let go of him altogether; at least not yet.

You have to understand. Grayson had become just as much a part of my life as Marc was. And on some crazy level, I had love for him. But by no means did I pull that particular problem out of the bag to have a closer look. Love was not part of the deal or my M.O.

When I started cutting back on my time with Grayson, he didn't complain because he had his own thing going on. I knew about his other woman and fully expected him to do his own thing. How could I expect him to be faithful to me, when I was sneaking around myself? I may not have turned my good thing completely a loose, but I decided I would do better by my husband. For once in our marriage, I was going to do my level best to please him.

I enrolled myself in college. Yeah, I didn't think I would do it either. I hadn't decided what I wanted to be or do. It was a big enough step for me just to get started. When I told Marc I was on my way to a college degree, he was over the moon. My husband's chest was stuck out so far, you would have thought I had set a world record or something. He did nothing but encourage me. He was so happy I made this step, he started catering to me. On the nights I had homework, he made sure I wasn't disturbed. Sometimes he would sit and rub my feet and bring me tea to relax me. Until that point, I didn't know how important it was for him to have a college-educated wife. And you know what? Even I got into the excitement.

It didn't take long before I found I liked higher learning and eventually chose a major. After having to take a computer class, I became fascinated with everything about them, so I decided to invest my time in computer science. Now you may think, because I previously had no interest in a college education that this was farfetched for me; not in the least. I never said I was dumb. But in fact, I graduated from high school with honors, with my best subject being math. How do you think I'm maintaining my wealth? Humph! I'm not a fool!

I got so good and so involved in my new major, even Grayson pitched in and helped. Instead of meeting for a night of loving, sometimes we would meet for him to tutor me on the subjects he was good at. Things in my life were going pretty well and I loved it! For once, home life and side life coincided harmoniously.

## Things never stay the same~

**For a few months, things sailed on smooth waters. I was happy.**

I was loving my new life as a college student, and my husband was slaying the business world with his expansions. There was nothing that I could have been more proud of than our coming together as a real family. Mind you, I still hadn't stopped seeing Grayson, at least not just for sex anyway. But the times we did do-the-do, had dwindled down to once a month. We both knew we would eventually stop our meetings altogether, and we both were fine with it.

As a result of my changing ways, I started being more of a wife to Marc. I had become more loving and more giving. I even stopped taking my birth control pills, even though I was still letting Grayson hit it. I just made sure it wasn't during the times I was most fertile. I still had that nightmare of winding up on somebody's talk show.

My husband and I made love like we did when we were first married. And this time around, it was better. For the first time ever, I was beginning to let my guard down. The man had proved his worthiness and I was going to give him his just rewards in every way possible.

Marc noticed the change in me right away, though he never actually questioned it. I think he was just glad our union had turned a corner for the better. He started coming home with expensive trinkets that displayed his love for me. Out of all the time we'd been married, the only real piece of jewelry I owned was my multi-carat wedding rings, so it was a nice surprise to be showered with diamonds and pearls just because.

But like most things, they slow to a crawl or come to an end altogether. I still wasn't pregnant, although I was off the pill. And after a while, we weren't making love as much as we had before. But I chalked that up to our busy and sometimes conflicting schedules. I was still pursuing my piece of paper and Marc was traveling more frequently. So with my classes, Sasha's extra-curricular activities, and my husband having his own responsibilities, our lives changed. Things had taken a sharp turn from the sweet journey we had plotted and we soon began to drift apart. I didn't worry though, it had to happen. Nothing really does stay the same. But with me liking my new and improved life, I vowed we would overcome this too.

## Proving me right and then some~

**Even though I suspected my husband to be a cheater at the beginning of our marriage, I wanted him to prove me wrong. And I thought he had.**

After witnessing what I thought were my husband's virtues, even with this latest hiccup, I was feeling really good about the progress I'd made in our marriage. I was ready to do almost anything to get things back on the road to righteousness. And I knew the first thing that had to go was my relationship with Grayson.

The guilt from my dubious lifestyle was eating me up, so it was time to put an end to the deceit and stop seeing Grayson permanently. It was way past time to make the very best of my relationship with my husband. After all, Marc had fought off the company whore and came running home to Mama, when he could have easily dropped his pants and stuck it to her. He deserved so much better than what I had done to him.

In ending things, I found I couldn't just cut ties with Grayson cold turkey. There is something to be said for those ties that bind. Ending our relationship over the phone was just out of the question. I needed to meet one last time for old time's sake; just like in that song, I needed to kiss and say goodbye. But there would be a whole lot more than just kissing going on. And just like in that song, in spite of everything, I couldn't lie; I would miss him. With all the time we spent together, he had a deep and special place in my heart.

To cut those binding ties, I chose a time when Marc would be out of town on business. So I planned a three-day weekend with 'Marlene'. Yes, three whole days. There was no way I could say goodbye to Grayson in one night. There had to be enough time to get it all in. I wanted to be filled to the bream with non-stop memories, so we had to do the thang up right! Remember, I wasn't ever going to see the man again. So I packed up Sasha and sent her off with my sister and Grayson and I met for our last hoorah.

While Grayson drove us to our spot, I breathed a sigh of relief. My betrayal was finally coming to a close and I was finally going to become a proper wife. I was going to be the wife I should have been in the very beginning. I had even made an appointment to see a fertility specialist to get the ball rolling on giving my husband that son he'd been crowing about. Me, Marc, Sasha, and the new baby were going to be a real family and not just one that looked good on paper.

Humph. I have to take a step back in wonderment at the tricks, or in this case, traps, life has in store for us. Just when you've worked everything out for the good of everybody, shit has a way of landing dead center of your plans; busting them up no matter how sincere you might be about them. And the thing that got in the way of the blueprint for our happiness was Marc himself. He did something so unexpected and so off the wall, I didn't even see it coming; couldn't have seen it coming. His treachery was so profound until this day I'm still reeling from its consequences.

Would you believe it? My husband got a chance to nail that slow assistant of his after all! At least that's what I thought when I witnessed that sorted mess in the hotel corridor. I'm still confused about most of what happened before the horrid incident because those involved really didn't tell the same story. To this day, I'm still not certain of, or could swear to, everything that man did, because of the shame attached; a shame that will have repercussions for years to come.

It was kind of funny how it all went down. Grayson and I had arrived at our spot and were about to get off the elevator when I spotted Marc playing grab ass with Slow-Moe, while she was trying to unlock the door to their suite.

Trying not to get caught ourselves, we quietly slipped back inside and peeped around the corner watching them. I'd been so busy trying to get my own shit in order and rid myself of the guilt, I'd completely forgotten my husband's lustful ache for this cow. But to be fair; I thought that temptation had been squashed, after the rejection of Miss Kelly "Loose Ass" Clay. I should have known better. But hold on to your weaves and wigs, it gets worse!

Watching Marc rub himself all up against that fat ass of hers, brought back the justification for my cheating in the first place. And I could have lived with that fact of his unfaithfulness if what happened next hadn't occurred.

It took so long for Marc's piece of tail to open the door, that it was opened from the inside—by none other than the hostess with the mostest from our wedding reception. To say I was shocked would have been a gross understatement. But Mama Lou always said, what was done in the dark would surely manage to come crawling its way out into the daylight. So that whole monologue on our wedding night, about him not screwing her or anybody else, was to put my mind at ease about what he was really up to; nailing the both of them.

Grayson and I watched them all greet each other with a kiss. I don't know who was more shocked at this scene, him or me. First Miss Hostess grabbed Slow-Moe for a kiss before Marc joined in on the fun and took his turn to tongue down the girl. I suspected my husband had hoe tendencies, but this was above and beyond anything I could have imagined coming from him. Even Grayson was in awe of his cousin's dubious actions. He didn't think Marc's stuck-up ass had it in him to do a threesome. That made two of us.

We stood there watching the hostess pull the two new arrivals into the room and close the door. Several minutes had passed before I realized I was no longer looking at the trio, but a closed whore-room door. My mind had taken flight in all sorts of directions at once. Needless to say, my appetite for Grayson was completely gone. Hell, I'd forgotten why we were even there in the first place! The mere fact that he was standing beside me vanished the moment I witnessed my husband with those two women. I was just so stunned. But that wouldn't be the only bombshell of the night.

The first shock was my reaction to the whole ugly mess. Why should I have cared if my loving husband was banging two women at a time when I was literally standing in an open elevator with my own tail for the night? What surprised me was the anger. Yet I had no right to be, I was flaming mad. I wanted to hurt somebody. I wanted somebody to feel pain. I wanted satisfaction and I wanted it right then and there!

And like a sign from heaven (or hell), the second elevator door popped open, bringing forth a room service waiter. I watched him push the heavily laden cart down the hall a piece, to my cheating husband's suite. From the looks of things, they planned to work up a hearty appetite in there. This made me angrier. Not thinking of anything but revenge, I stepped from my hiding place and marched right down that hallway with Grayson in tow. He never tried to stop me. I guess he was curious to see what I was up to. But in hindsight, we both should have beat it back to his car, because what happened next blew the lid off of everything. Sometimes ignorance really is bliss.

As soon as the door opened from inside, I pushed past the waiter and the startled hostess, into the suite. High-stepping it towards the sounds of some happy soul being well satisfied, I rounded a corner to an open door and what I found was contemptible. Not only was there a third woman in this ménage a trio, but a second man. And there was my husband, at the foot of the bed, on his knees, thoroughly sucking the other man's cock.

Now out of all the scenarios I could have run through my head, this was certainly not one of them. I fully expected one woman to be on the king-sized bed with my husband, not two other women. But there they were in the middle of the bed; not even concerned about what was happening at the foot of it, because they had their own sucking and slurping thing going on.

I skidded to a complete stop at the sight of Marc with a dick in his mouth. He was so into pleasing this man, who had his head thrown back in complete ecstasy, that he never heard me enter the room. And I guess Miss Hostess saw the handwriting on the wall because she slipped in long enough to retrieve her clothing and fled the scene without informing the others of the impending trouble.

I couldn't move. I certainly couldn't utter a word. I just stood there watching my husband woman-handle this man. The more I saw, the darker the room became. Something was wrong with me, but my mind couldn't register what it was until my legs gave way. I had forgotten all about Grayson until I heard a perplexed 'What the fuck' behind me. And it was a good thing he was there too, or I would have hit the floor. He caught me when I passed out.

When I came around, my husband was scrambling around the room looking for his own clothes. The man he had been sucking off had donned his, and was limping out the door; trying to put on his other shoe. And as for Marc's assistant and the other woman, they were cowering on the bed clutching each other for safety I suppose.

Grayson helped me to my feet. I watched Marc, who couldn't make eye contact with me or Grayson, pull on his pants. That's when I flew into him. I slapped, kicked, and cursed at him; all the while he tried to protect himself from my blows. The two women took this as their cue to grab whatever they could and sprint for the exit. I guess they figured they would be next and they would have been correct. I had a few licks for whoever was left after I had my satisfaction with my husband.

Grayson let me have my say with my fists for a while, before picking me up and carrying me out of the suite past the still startled waiter who had come inside to witness the drama. By this time, there was so much commotion, that several occupants on that floor had ventured out of their hidey-holes, to see what all the fuss was about. I was still cursing and screaming when the elevator doors slid shut. Grayson didn't put me down until we were in the underground garage and at his car. It took everything in him to keep me from sprinting back onto that elevator and back to that asshole's room.

## The Aftermath~

**In the end, Marc did get one up on me…well, in fact, four, if you count all of those women along with the encounter with that man. And I especially count that man, viciously!**

I have to count him. Because that man and God only knows how many more before him, is the reason why I'm sitting in my doctor's office waiting on results from my second HIV test. Marc wasn't practicing safe sex when it came to his encounters. And I call them encounters because I refused to accept them as being anything more than that. It wasn't like what I had with Grayson, a one-on-one relationship. My husband had too many people involved for them to be called relationships.

But the thing that got me the most was his haphazard behavior during those encounters. It was bad enough he was screwing those women without a condom, but he was screwing, (and yes he did that too), his male partner, or partners, without one too. He didn't bother to protect himself, let alone me.

I believe in living and letting others live and don't judge people for their preferences or behaviors. How can I when I wasn't right myself? But to say I wasn't disturbed by my husband's behavior with that man would have been a lie. When I married Marc, I fully expected to be in a heterosexual relationship, not in one with a husband who liked men too. He could have been gay or bi or whatever, all he wanted; but just should have left me out of it. I never will understand why he married me in the first place.

After hell broke out in that hotel suite, I've had to reevaluate so many things in my life. My husband's behavior threw me farther than I thought possible. I had never been on the receiving end of a plot twist that huge and heavy. I have always been the one to dish out the pain, but not this time. All those times he was trying to keep an eye on me, he had to be whoring around. He needed to know where I was so I wouldn't walk up on him. Humph, so much for that!

Grayson brought me back to the house that night and stayed with me. Neither of us expected Marc to come back there and he didn't. And if the truth were to be told, I didn't care one way or the other. I didn't care if he came home to find his cousin in our bed comforting me. It may have been a surprise to him or maybe not, I don't know. In the midst of all that commotion, I don't think Marc even realized Grayson was there or that we were together. At this point, I don't think it much matters.

A few days later, he sent for his things, which consisted of his clothes, a few odds and ends, and all of his business papers. He was specific about what he wanted taken from the house even though most of the stuff there were his purchases. Marc was the one to furnish our home. I just nodded and agreed during the whole process.

Remember, I never expected our marriage to be a permanent one anyway. But it was as if he was afraid to ask for any more than those items. He had someone to come in, box everything up, and move them out. They never said where they were taking his things and I never asked.

I stayed in our home for days on end after that; trying to make some sense of not only Marc's behavior but mine too. I looked back and saw the arrogance that I had heavily accused my husband of possessing within myself. But truth be told, I was worse than him. My attitude was to always get him before he got me. I was never fair, not even once. But then again, in the end, neither was he. Neither one of us had any business in a marriage. Where Marc was being who he was, (although despicably), I was running roughshod over not only him but every man who managed to cross my path, maybe with the exception of Grayson Hill.

When Marc finally did rise from his hidey-hole, he did so by phone. I listened, while he awkwardly tried to make polite conversation, but after his words fell on numb ears, he switched gears; stating that he never meant for things to turn out the way they did.

In Marc speak, that meant he never meant to get caught. He hurriedly babbled about something or other; never allowing space for me to say anything or ask any questions. Surprisingly, he never asked me any questions either. Like, why was I even there that night? But in all, he said, not one time did he apologize or ask for forgiveness. He never offered a true explanation for what happened that night, nothing.

I marveled at the fact he didn't ask for my forgiveness. That said to me, he didn't much care if he had it or not. Another thing that struck me, he didn't mention anything about Grayson and me or anything else that I'd done. Not one time did he bring up my scandal with his cousin, and to this day I don't know if he knew about us or not. If he did; he kept it to himself and probably figured his transgressions were way worse than mine.

There was one thing that he did ask of me. He asked that I never reveal to anyone what happened that night and in exchange, he would give me anything I wanted in our divorce settlement. He was more concerned about his reputation being tarnished than he was about anything else.

Strange. In the midst of it all, until he uttered those words 'divorce' and 'settlement', divorce had never crossed my mind. He just took it for granted that was the only solution. And he was correct. Even though I hadn't thought about it, there was no way we could have stayed together, not even for Sasha's sake.

And speaking of Sasha. That child's heart was broken in two when Marc disappeared from our lives. I thought he would have at least phoned her from time to time, but he didn't. My baby girl was the one hurt most out of our mess. And even stranger, up until that point I never considered how my behavior towards Marc, towards men in general would affect my girl.

I have a lot to answer for. In my rush to punish all men for what my daddy did to Mama Lou before I was born, I had hurt the one person I was supposed to protect—my child.

Marlene and Grayson both have been mighty good to me and Sasha. They have checked up on us and relayed messages that needed relaying between myself and Marc. There was a good thing that came out of this mess. The cousins were talking again and not just Marlene and Marc, but Grayson too. After that night, he gave up his grudge against Marc and invested in some act right of his own. The reality had set in that anyone of us could be in my situation. But it didn't stop Marlene's side business though. She just put more safeguards in place to prevent drama and potential tragedy.

And as you can see, I've talked more about my baby girl since all of this has happened. I've finally put her where she should have been all along, first! When it came to my life, my child had been mostly along for the ride. I had selfishly placed her to the side, only focusing on her when it suited me. And for that, I am most ashamed. And Mama Lou would certainly be ashamed of me. If there was one thing she did do, it was to make sure Amber and I were first and foremost in her life. Now I'm beginning to see why she never dated or married again. She put all of her focus on raising us girls to be the best we could be, and I failed her. But I won't be making that mistake again. I have a lot to make up for…that is if time allows me.

Grayson and I are not together anymore, but we're still the best of friends. Now that Marc and I are in the middle of a divorce, he comes around regularly without Marlene's wigs (smile). He and his lady friend are seriously considering getting married. I'm happy for him. Somebody needs to make good after all this mess. I don't blame him

for anything that happened with me. I was the one who had

a commitment with Marc and should have stayed true to it.

I often wondered what would have happened if we never

went to that hotel that night. Would Marc and I still be

together? I guess we will never know.

Marc never came back to our house after that night.

He moved into one of his many properties, which some, I

will soon own after the divorce is final. Even though we

were supposed to leave with what we came in with, Marc

agreed to give me whatever I wanted, to keep my mouth

shut about his proclivities for men. That little tidbit of

information would quickly sink his business in one

whopping swoop if his peers ever found out. I was

generous though. I only asked for our house and a couple of

other properties. One being the one I grew up in with

Amber and Mama Lou. For whatever reason, Marc never

sold the place but did manage to turn it into one hell of a

showplace. This made me realize Amber and I should never have let it go in the first place. I had come full circle.

I still attend college. And come what may, I plan to graduate and with honors, thank you very much. I want to start my own business. Something that will keep me occupied and not let me slip back into my old pattern of behavior, although I don't think there is a chance of that ever happening. I've learned my lesson. This episode with Marc has cured me of my man-bashing and lying ways. I'm all about living a clean respectable life, and not so much for myself, but for my daughter.

I hate it took all of this for me to make this change. My foolishness had many consequences, with the greatest being Sasha could lose me if just one of these tests should come back positive. It would be a case of the sins of a parent visiting a child and all of that. I did listen to Mama Lou, even if I didn't practice much of what she taught me.

I still have to shake my head in fascination with the irony of it all. Here I was thinking I was getting over on Marc and he was getting over on me big time. And to top it all off, he may have started the slow process of killing me with a deadly disease. I haven't talked much to him since all of this happened, but he has assured me, through Marlene, that everyone involved in that night is clean. How can I trust that when he didn't protect himself? And what about the people I don't know about?

In all of my plotting and playing, I never considered an end game, and certainly not one that could end my life. What can I say? I was all up for a little tit-for-tat in the cheating game, but I never signed on for a switch-hitting husband. I never guessed once he was into men as well as women. What straight woman would think that? Especially after all the loving he and I had.

So, I guess you can say the joke is on me. And you also may say I brought it all on myself and I would have to agree with you. I wish I could say Mama should have warned us about these types of events while she was telling us everything else, but I guess she lived in a time when she didn't have to worry about such things. I should have been aware though. I knew what it was like out here. But I thought my husband with all his sense had the sense to look out for himself and protect us both. I sure did with Grayson and every man I was with before him.

Yeah, I should have been vigilant against the unknown. That's what gets you every time. That something out of the blue that can stumble in and ruin your life forever. It's that one left-out piece of information that can set your world on fire for the wrong reasons.

Well, my doctor is back with my test results. I pray that I'm still negative and can breathe a sigh of calm relief—until the next one. And if it is negative, I will have to do this dance again a few more times before I can breathe for real. **Wish me luck!**